Annabelle Alpaca
Plants a Garden

Written by
Jan O'Neill
text copyright ©2003

Illustrated by B.E. Anderson
illustration copyright ©2003

Dedicated to Richard for believing in the dream.

My deepest appreciation goes to Bonnie and Judy
for their endless assistance. J.O.

Dedicated to Dad and David who helped me be. B.A.

It was the end of a long cold winter. Annabelle, a Suri (SUR-ee) alpaca, was in the barn talking to her barnyard friends. Ebony, a shiny black chicken, was searching through the dirt for a kernel of corn. "Oh Annabelle, I wish there was a fresh tomato to eat. I am so tired of the same dried corn."

As Annabelle looked in the stall, there was Banner, an Arabian horse, munching on hay. "I wish I had a fresh carrot to nibble on," he said to Annabelle. "I have eaten hay all winter."

Annabelle looked up and coming at her was an old paper bag rolling off the hay stack. As it hit the barn floor, she jumped out of the way and out tumbled Tag, the kitten. "Oh, hi Tag," Annabelle said. "You scared me for a minute. I thought that bag was alive!"

"I'm sorry," said Tag. "I am bored with winter. It's been so dull and gray outside for so long now. I can't wait for spring to get here. Fresh catnip in the spring is so good."

Annabelle couldn't stop thinking about the taste of fresh carrots, cabbage and lettuc
All of her favorite foods. She strolled outside and bumped into Marshmallow Fluff,
Huacaya (wa-KAI-ya) alpaca friend of hers. "Oh, sorry Fluff, I was daydreaming abou
spring and I didn't see you," hummed Annabelle.

Spring?! Spring! Spring is almost here, yippee!" said Fluff she jumped into the air.

"You're right Fluff, it is almost here. I can feel the warm sun on my fleece and the little shoots of grass are popping out of the ground!" exclaimed Annabelle. "Fluff, wouldn't it be fun to do something special to celebrate spring?" she asked.

"What could we do?" asked Fluff. "I don't know much about spring since I am only ten months old."

Annabelle was six years old and remembered many of the joys of spring. "Spring is a time for new things, Fluff. Alpaca crias can be born in the spring and chicks hatch from their eggs in the spring. Also, colorful flowers begin to grow and the earth changes from gray to green," explained Annabelle.

"I've got it!" shouted Annabelle. "I know how we can celebrate spring!   We can plant a garden!"

"A garden, what is that?" asked Fluff.

"A garden is a place where vegetables like carrots, lettuce and corn grow," said Annabelle.

♪ "Yes, let's plant a garden, let's plant a garden," sang Fluff as she skipped through the barn.

Banner's ears perked up as he heard Fluff's song. "I will help you plant a garden Annabelle," said Banner.

Ebony came running towards Banner's stall. "Garden? garden? did somebody say garden?" asked Ebony.

"Yes, Ebony," said Annabelle, "we are going to plant a garden. Do you want to help?"

"Yes, yes , yes, I want to help," clucked Ebony. "I can plant the seeds."

Tag was sleeping in the pail, when he heard all of the excitement. He woke up and lazily stretched his legs. "What's going on?" asked Tag.

"We're planting a garden. Do you want to help too?" asked Annabelle.

"Can we plant some catnip?" Tag purred.

"Sure we can, if you will help," said Banner.

During the next few days, the sun warmed the earth around Annabelle's barn. The barnyard friends were busy gathering tools and supplies for their garden. "I've got the seeds," Ebony called.

"I found a plow to make the rows," Banner neighed.

"That's good," said Annabelle. "Fluff and I have been busy making row markers and Tag found a watering can."

"Before we head out to the garden, I have a present for all of you," she said. Annabelle pulled out a big bag with brightly colored hats and bandanna's. "Let's get in the mood for spring by wearing something cheerful," said Annabelle.

"What a fun idea," nickered Banner as he pulled a golden yellow hat out of the bag.

After all the friends had picked out something to wear, and helped each other put them on, something magical happened. Each of the animals began to change color. Banner turned a bright gold, Tag became lavender, Ebony became a shiny blue chicken. Fluff jumped in excitement as she saw Annabelles locks turn rose as Banner tied a bright pink bandanna around her neck.

Look Annabelle, shouted Fluff, everyone is turning the color of spring.

Isn' t it wonderful Fluff, said Annabelle.

The friends formed a circle and marveled at their newly colored coats, fleeces, feathers and furs. "Look at Fluff! She has turned into the brightest white huacaya I have ever seen!" Annabelle exclaimed.

"Thank you Annabelle," nickered Banner, "for my new hat and gold coat!"

"Yes, thank you," added all the other animals.

"You are all welcome," answered Annabelle. "It really feels like spring is finally here. Let's go plant the garden, while the sun is still shining."

The friends set out for the open field, prancing proudly in their spring attire and their newly colored coats, fleeces, feathers and furs. Banner pulled the plow while Ebony and Tag hitched a ride. Fluff and Annabelle followed closely behind.

"Be sure to make the rows straight!" Annabelle reminded Banner. Ebony moved through the rows pushing one seed at a time into the warm earth with her beak.

"Tag, it will be your job to cover the seeds," instructed Annabelle. Fluff and Annabelle placed a colorful marker at the end of each row.

"Corn, carrots, peas, radishes, lettuce, tomatoes, cabbage, and beans," Fluff read.

"Don't forget the catnip," meowed Tag. "You promised to plant some!"

"We did promise, Tag. We will make one more row for the catnip," replied Banner.

Together, Banner, Fluff, and Annabelle took turns hauling water from the barn to the garden. When all the rows were planted, covered, watered, and marked, the friends stood back and admired their work.

Several days later, Annabelle came running to the barn, with her long spiral loc glistening in the sun as she moved. "Banner? Ebony? Tag? Are you in there?" she calle

Fluff came running up bumping into Annabelle as she tried to stop. "Is something wror Annabelle?" asked Fluff.

"Quite the opposite," she beamed. "Everything is right. It's sunny, it's spring time, ar the first radish seedlings have poked through the soil."

"Let's go see the garden!" Banner exclaimed and off he trotted, followed by Ebor flapping her wings as she ran.

All through the summer Annabelle and her friends watered and weeded their garden. In the evenings, they would rest by the garden edge and watch in amazement as the plants seemed to grow before their very eyes.

Soon, the leaves on the trees began to turn to orange and red. Annabelle called to her friends, "It is time to harvest the garden."

The friends spent the day picking corn, carrots, peas, radishes, lettuce, tomatoes, cabbage and beans. They carried all of the bounty to the barn in baskets and pails.

That evening, Annabelle, Ebony, Fluff, Tag and Banner invited all of the animals from the barn to share in their feast. As Annabelle looked around the barn, she was delighted at what she saw. Banner and the other horses were enjoying the taste of fresh carrots. The hens joined Ebony in sharing a bright red tomato. Fluff and her alpaca friends munched on cabbage, lettuce and fresh carrots.

Everyone was happy and thankful that all of their hard work during the spring and the summer had paid off.

Annabelle was about to join in on the feast, but first she had to find Tag. Where was Tag???

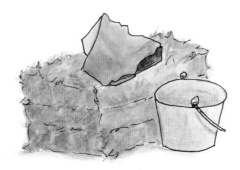